I0553527

FINDING

PURPOSE:

Boogie's Story

By Mark L Baynard

Finding Purpose
Copyright © 2018 – Mark L Baynard

2018 © In Pursuit of Freedom Publishing

Printed in the United States

The is a fictional book and doesn't depict any person, places, or situations. Any similarities between characters or situations are unintentional or co-incidental!

ISBN 13: 978-0-9861380-3-4

ISBN 10: 0986138037

Library of Congress Control Number 2018902168

Editor: Mark Baynard, In Pursuit of Freedom Publishing
Book Cover Design: Ida Jannson for Amygdala Designs, amagdaladesign.net

Contact Information: mark100years@yahoo.com
Website: www.journey100years.com

<u>**Books by The Author: Mark L Baynard**</u>
100 Years: A Journey to End a Vicious Cycle
These Are Your Flowers (Life Has Meaning Series)
100 Years II: Truth Be Told
Finding Purpose: Boogie's Story

Social Networks:
Twitter: www.twitter.com/mark100years
Facebook Page www.facebook.com/mark100years
Facebook Page: www.facebook.com/journey100years
YouTube http://www.youtube.com/c/MarkBaynard
Author Page: www.amazon.com/-/e/B00TLXK5L6
LinkedIn: www.linkedin.com/in/MarkBaynard
Goodreads www.goodreads.com/mark100years
Instagram www.instagram.com/mark100years
Pinterest: www.pinterest.com/mark100years
Periscope www.periscope.tv/mark100years
Google+ @mark100years

In Pursuit of Freedom Publishing

When considering life and all that it means, many questions come to my mind. In the process of answering those questions, I began to find purpose.

Mark L Baynard

"Finding Purpose"

www.journey100years.com

FINDING

PURPOSE

Table of Contents

Dedication

This book is dedicated to anyone who faced challenges in their life. I understand that life may be difficult and full of surprises. I hope that this story will inspire others to find purpose and/or meaning in their life. It's not about what we go through in life but more about how we rise back to our feet. The "Most High God" has given us the strength to endure until the end. Continue to stand strong brothers & sisters and witness the power of God.

Introduction

Finding Purpose: Boogie's Story is a fictional story full of some of the challenges faced by most teenagers. Boogie is a 17-year-old inner-city teenager who was raised by his single mother. Being a teenager, he must deal with peer pressure and other challenges. His mother works hard to take care of him and guide him in the right direction. Being a single parent may be difficult, but she is prepared to fight until the end for her son. She refuses to go down without a fight. Boogie was taught to be respectful to others but will stand his ground to survive in his reality.

Boogie finds himself caught in a dilemma. His dilemma consists of waiting patiently to get hired on a job or earning money the quick way. Though the second option sounds more appealing, it comes with a price. Boogie has goals of becoming a responsible man but doesn't appear to be headed in that direction yet.

There is nothing new or unusual about this, as difficult decisions are made each day. Here's a few examples: A mother must decide whether to keep her child or have an abortion. A father must decide whether to stand up and be responsible for his child or run from his responsibilities. This may sometimes include choosing to sacrifice the pleasures of the streets and being a responsible parent. Boogie's challenge will be whether he is able to make the right decision at the right time.

It is believed that when we find purpose and meaning in our lives, we are more likely to become successful. One of the goals of the author of this book is to enhance our quality of life as humans. Though many things could go wrong during our learning and growing process in life, the rewards are great. We must know that everyone who goes through the process doesn't make it through.

When thinking about life and everything that we see around us, several questions may come to mind. This book will allow sparks of thought to enter our minds. Questions such as; why are we here? What is our life all about? Will things get better for us or is our current life all there is to look forward to? Why, why, and why? This can become a frustrating part of the process for anyone. Seems to be more questions than answers. Though frustrating, it has the potential of adding growth to our lives.

In this book we will see the journey through the eyes of Boogie. Let's see how he deals with life as a teenager.

FINDING

PURPOSE

Finding Purpose

Chapter 1

What is It?

Loud sirens, police radio's, and the sound of

tires from patrol cars racing down the street

could be heard as officers chase the suspect.

"The suspect is wearing a black sweat -hood,

blue jeans, and white sneakers." This could be heard coming across the police radio. "The suspect is a black male between 5 feet 11 inches and 6 feet 2 inches tall. He is running down 21st street north headed towards 22nd. He appears to have something in his right hand. He is considered armed and dangerous."

Boogie, a young confused black male, was running as fast as he could. Fearful of getting caught, Boogie jumped a fence and ran through an alley. He ran across the street, almost got hit by a car. "That was a close call," Boogie thought to himself. Boogie didn't want to return to juvenile detention again, under any

circumstances.

Boogie had previously been in juvenile

detention twice already. The thought alone of

returning made him sick to his stomach. The

first time he was arrested on a simple possession

of marijuana charge. The marijuana was found

in his front pocket. He served thirty days in

juvenile detention on that arrest and

adjudication. The second time he was arrested

on an intent-to-sell-marijuana charge. Boogie

had a few goals and returning to lock-up wasn't

one of them. Boogie hated that he had no

control of his own life while in juvie. He was

happy to be out of juvenile detention and

wanted to make something good out of his life.

After serving a six-month sentence, Boogie was

released and started serving a six-month

probation sentence. Boogie appeared to be doing

well for the first five months. He had a good

relationship with his probation officer. He was

on time when making all his appointments with

his probation officer. He was glad to submit to

several drugs test. Boogie's urinalysis test

always came back clean. Boogie continued

doing well until the last month of his probation

sentence.

While running from the police Boogie knew there may be consequences ahead. If he got arrested, he would most likely return to what he referred to as "the hell hole."

The officer started gaining on Boogie and giving a play-by-play description of the events. "The suspect is running through the alleyway on Gamble Street and will come out on Capitol Avenue between 30th and 31st street." Boogie noticed that the sounds of police sirens and radios were getting louder as additional patrol cars joined the chase. The flashing red and blue lights from the patrol cars lit the streets up like a parade or something. Curious bystanders started

to flood the streets wanting to see the action.
Some of them pulled out their cell phones,
tablets, and devices & started recording the
melee. Boogie heard one of the officers yell out
things like "stop, give yourself up, and you
won't get away." Boogie wasn't hearing any of
that nonsense. Boogie also thought that there
was a chance that he may get beaten by officers
for running. He's seen it several times in his
neighborhood and on the news. Someone in the
crowd could be heard yelling "worldstar!" "I'm
putting this chase on worldstar."

As Boogie ran away from the police, he had an
extra boost of energy. Boogie wiped his face,

causing sweat to gush from his hand. Sweat

continued running down his face. He also

remembered what the Judge last said to him.

Judge Hardball told Boogie that he would throw

the book at him if he ever came back in his

courtroom. Judge Hardball was hard but fair.

Though Judge Hardball was known for handing

down harsh sentences to repeat offenders, he

believed in second chances.

Second chances were one thing, but what about

third chances. If caught, this would be Boogie's

third run-in with the law. Not everyone believes

in third chances. Boogie being a repeat offender,

knew that he could possibly be given a harsher

sentence. There was even a chance that Boogie would be charged as an adult. Boogie was 17 years old but the fact that his eighteenth birthday was only days away, didn't help matters.

While running away from the officers, Boogie threw something to the ground. "I hope that they didn't see me throw it," Boogie thought to himself as he ran. Boogie didn't have a plan or strategy of how he was going to get away, he just ran. Returning to a juvenile detention center did not sound good to him at all.

Yes, others may say that Boogie shouldn't have committed the crime if he didn't want to return to juvenile. As the old saying goes "if you can't

do the time, don't do the crime. That's a true

statement but Boogie wasn't hearing that at the

time. Especially, while caught up in the streets.

Boogie wasn't thinking on that level. He didn't

always use the best process for decision making.

As he continued to run, he was starting to breath

heavily and began panting. Boogie was starting

to get tired but getting locked up wasn't an

option for him so he continued. Boogie just

wanted to get away from the cops. Boogie didn't

want his story to end like this.

Though he was getting tired, he continued to

run. He ran, and ran, and ran! The only thing

that he thought of was that he had to continue to run. As he ran, he did something that he doesn't normally do. He started to think! Yes, he thought about things in the past, but this was different. Boogie began to think about more serious things that he hadn't previously thought about. It was like, his life was in a bottle. Running and thinking, thinking and running, running and thinking, thinking and running; such an awakening thing to do. It was as if time suddenly stopped for Boogie. Boogie saw his life flash before his eyes. All the mistakes that he ever made. All the wrong that he'd done. The good, the bad, and the ugly stood before his eyes. Such a sobering moment at the most inconvenient time. The light was now on, in his head.

"Why am I here? What is life all about? Will things get better for me or is this all that I have to look forward to?" Things such as what, where, when, how and why concerning his life; came to Boogie's mind. He thought about his mother and all her many encouraging words about getting his life together. He remembered the words that his mother spoke to him prior to leaving the house that morning. "Something good is going to happen for you today so don't mess it up." So many thoughts were running through Boogie's mind. Thoughts such as these can become frustrating for a teenager to deal with, but they had a different effect on Boogie. These thoughts were sobering for Boogie. Boogie felt like he was standing in front of a Judge whom he couldn't lie to nor deceive. Boogie felt exposed and knew that he could no longer hid behind lies. Boogie started feeling several different emotions such as guilt, doubt, and fear. This may sound crazy, but Boogie was also feeling the greatest emotion, love! Yes, Love! Boogie felt a strong sense of the love that his mother has for him. Boogie also felt the love that the creator of the universe has for all mankind. For some reason, Boogie was open to the information that he was getting. As these thoughts flashed before his eyes, he began to think that there must be more to life.

Boogie thought about Tameka! Tameka was Boogie's girlfriend. Though Boogie didn't always show it, Tameka had a special place in his heart. Out of all the women that he knew, Tameka was second only to his mother. Boogie thought about all the pain that he caused Tameka. He also wondered if Tameka would stand by his side, if he were to get arrested again. Tameka held Boogie down every time he went through anything, even while in juvenile detention. Tameka was his ride or die chick. Boogie thought of the many good times that he shared with Tameka. When Boogie and Tameka where only eight years old, they used to play on the merry-go-round in the park. Boogie would run fast next to the merry-go-round, while pushing with Tameka on it, and then jump on. They would laugh and have the most fun. Boogie shared his first kiss ever with Tameka.

Boogie also thought about Misty. Misty was fun to be around and full of excitement. She was down for anything. Boogie liked that Misty was willing to go further than a kiss. Boy he had fun times with Misty. Misty was his homegirl. The main drawback that Boogie felt when it came to Misty was that she came with extra. Yes, extra!

Extra attitude, extra baggage, and extra

heartache. Boogie thought of the many good

times that they had together. Boogie then had a

slight frown on his face, as he wondered why

Misty seemed to fade away while he was in

detention.

Boogie also considered the fact that his mother

liked Tameka a bit more than she liked Misty.

She considered Misty to be slightly fast for a

girl her age. Tameka knew how to reach

Boogie's soft spot. Yes, he had a soft spot for

Tameka. He trusted Tameka with some of his

personal secrets. Boogie shared some very

personal things with Tameka. She never threw those things back in his face.

As Boogie continued to run, for some reason, he felt a sense of peace, as if something was going to change in his life for the better. Boogie then had a quick thought and drifted into some of his most pleasant dreams. He thought about going on his dream vacation, driving through town with the car of his dreams, and living in his dream home. He didn't know why he would think of these things at a time like this. Those pleasant thoughts quickly left his mind as he came back to reality. Well, the truth was that his current situation was not a good look for him at all. One thing that Boogie was starting to understand clearer was that there will be consequences for his actions. There's no way around it.

Boogie thought about stopping but then thought against it. Boogie felt that if he were to get caught, the officers would have to catch him themselves. No freebees for them, Boogie thought. His mind then shifted to some of the events that led to this moment. It started about one week ago!

Chapter 2

A Week Ago!

It was warm outside to start the morning and the
weatherman reported that it was going to be a
hot one! One thing about the city is that
something usually goes wrong during those hot
summer days. Many people were expected to be

in the streets during this hot summer day. The local parks would be filled with teenagers playing basketball, handball, and football. The girls would be jumping rope and playing hopscotch. Other girls would just be standing around looking cute and checking out the boys. All the girls and guys were expected to be out in full force, looking to impress the other. The summer was starting out with a bang. The forecast for the week, was expected to be hot! It was going to be "on and popping."

"Wake up, wake up; get out of that bed!" Yelled Boogie's mother, as she banged on his bedroom door. He was most likely having a peaceful dream as he slept. "It's time to get up and get ready for the job fair," shouted Boogie's mother.

Boogie's mother was an honest woman and a very hard worker. She only wanted what she thought was best for her son. She always taught him to do the right thing. "Don't steal, respect your elders, treat all people as you want to be treated, and tell the truth" were some of her expectations. Yes, she taught Boogie some of those good old fashion values. Though she didn't go to church each week, she prayed for her son daily.

Though Boogie didn't have a job, his mother encouraged him to look for a job each day. She also had vocally disagreed with his current lifestyle of being in the street. You may say that Boogie was also a hustler. Boogie was not a major hustler but more of a part-time hustler who would find a way of making money. Boogie did everything from shoveling snow in the winter to cutting grass in the summer. Boogie also tried his hand at selling marijuana here and there to make extra money.

His mother worked at the local bakery. She proudly had her High School Diploma on the wall in her living room. Beside raising Boogie, earning her High School Diploma was one of her greatest accomplishment. She excitedly tells the story of how she studied daily to earn her

High School Diploma. Boogie's mother didn't

play when it came to him going to school and

earning an education. Boogie remembers the

many times that his mother told him that earning

a High School Diploma was a must for him.

Boogie was proud of his mother and the

example that she set for him. Boogie's mother

picked-up her baking skill while in her High

School's home economics class. She just

continued to develop her skills into one of the

best bakers in her town. She was known for

baking cakes for birthday parties, weddings, and

anniversaries on the side. She did this to earn

extra money to help raise her son. She would do anything for her son Boogie. Boogie knew that his mother loved him, but he didn't always show her just how much he really appreciated her.

Some critics may ask why she put up with his criminal lifestyle. The truth of the matter is she was totally against it. Boogie's mother didn't support him selling drugs at all. She was a realest and knew, as a mother, there were several options at her disposal to reach her son. One option would be to put her son out of her house and let him learn the hard way. This is the old-school tough love mentality. Secondly, she could constantly nag him and tell him all the things that he was doing wrong. The third option

would be to encourage her son to make better

decisions and kind of show him the way.

Boogie's mother thought that putting her son out

in the streets, knowing all the elements out

there, may be something that she would later

regret. Nagging her teenage son may eventually

push him further into the streets.

Boogie's mother selected the third and probably

the most effective option for her. She chose to

continue to encourage him to get it right and

make better decisions. She also figured that by

setting a good example for him to follow would

increase her son's chances making a change. In

addition to this, Boogie's mother believed that her prayers for him would be answered. This is something that she did privately as she asked God to show her son the way and spare him from the many dangers in the street.

Though Boogie's mother wasn't a religious fanatic, her actions and faith in God was commendable. This may put her in the category of being a Christian. She thought that by loving and supporting her son would give Boogie the best chance to succeed. Boogie's mother knew about the dangers of the streets and didn't want her son to fall victim to any of that. His mother also experienced the death of her brother Gus,

Boogie's Uncle. Boogie heard many stories about his Uncle Gus.

Ten minutes went by and Boogie's mother returned and didn't hear any movement in his bedroom. She yelled and banged for him to get out of the bed. Boogie responded, "alright mom," but did not move a muscle. His mother continued to bang and yell louder until she heard movement. "Alright already, mom I'm getting up." Boogie slowly proceeded to move out of his bed. Boogie yarned and stretched a little to wake-up.

His mother had ironed his clothes the night before to ensure that he looked presentable and dressed business professional. Boogie had on a suit, a tie and dress shoes. He had a folder with several copies of his resume. He was prepared and ready to start work that day, if possible.

His resume listed the volunteer work he did and the summer jobs that he previously held. Boogie's mother took pictures and told her son that he looked nice while dressed up.

Boogie wasn't a bad kid; he just needed some guidance. His Uncle used to say things like "this child is going become something great." Boogie missed his Uncle Gus, as he was one of only a few positive male role models that he knew. Boogie heard many good stories of how his

Uncle helped his mother any time she needed him. His Uncle Gus didn't have much money as he worked as a laborer construction worker.

Boogie may have inherited a good work ethic from his uncle. He did whatever he could to earn extra money. Boogie's uncle wouldn't have agreed with his lifestyle. His mother continually warned him many times of the dangers of the streets. It was necessary for Boogie to learn some things about life the hard way. She just prayed that his life would be spared.

The job fair was at the civic center and it was packed. There were thousands of people there looking for work. Most booths had long lines of people. Boogie was prepared and waited patiently in line. While at the job fair, Boogie stopped at several different booths and spoke to potential employers. He also filled out several job applications on the spot. He gave out several resumes to different employers. He seemed to be prepared for some of the questions. The day prior to the job fair, Boogie practiced some of the potential questions with his mother.

Boogie felt good about his conversation with Mr. Johnson. Mr. Johnson was the representative from a local fast food restaurant. Boogie shared about how he was a hard worker and could be relied upon to arrive to work on time and get the job done. He then went to visit other booths.

Boogie suddenly noticed a familiar face. It was his school counselor. "Hey counselor Wilson, said Boogie! How are you doing?" "I'm good, responded Mr. Wilson, How are you?" Boogie laughingly replied, "I'm trying to get a job." After giving Boogie a few pointers, Counselor Wilson wished Boogie well and they walked in different directions. Boogie then waited in another long line and filled out another job application.

"Ring," "ring," "ring," blasted from Boogie's phone as he realized that he forgot to turn off his cell phone. He quickly pushed the vibrate button. "Vibrate," "vibrate," "vibrate" as the employer gave Boogie an odd stare. Boogie shrugged his shoulders and continued to the next booth. He met several potential employers and felt good about his chances. Though he felt good about his chances of getting hired for a job, he also knew that his past may hold him back. Having an arrest record has the potential of hurting his chances. The job fair was a good experience for Boogie, but he knew there were no promises.

Boogie then went to see Fred. Fred is not only

Boogie's friend, but he's his best friend.

They've been friends since elementary school.

Fred was Boogie's first friend in the

neighborhood. They were in some of the same

classes in school. They went to gym classes

together and played on some of the same little

league teams. When you saw Boogie, Fred was

not far behind. They shared a few laughs as

usual. Boogie told Fred everything that

happened at the job fair.

FINDING

PURPOSE

Chapter 3

You Can Run

The sound of Boogie's cell phone "ringtone,

ringtone, ringtone." He knew that this was his

girlfriend "Tameka." Tameka's personal

ringtone blared through his phone's speaker.

Boogie had all intentions of returning Tameka's

call as soon as possible. Though he planned to call her after he finished, he quickly forgot. This time he had a good excuse. Boogie forgot as he got caught up trying to get a job while at the fair. She would be sure to forgive him for that. He answered the phone in a pleasant voice "hello sweetheart!" She responded with a "I'm good." Where you at, she asked? Boogie then responded by saying "I'm hanging out with Fred." Why didn't you answer your phone, she asked? Oh yea, I almost forgot to tell you that I went to the job fair. She asked if he found a job and he responded by saying "I'm not sure!" Boogie's girlfriend Tameka was about to get off work. She worked part-time at a local department store downtown. Tameka told Boogie that she loved him and asked him to come over when he gets a chance. Boogie said that he would be sure to try.

Boogie decided to head to the famous Walton's Chicken spot on the Avenue to get a two-piece special. Walton's Chicken is a popular restaurant and may be the best chicken in town. Their food has a special taste to it. They have a secret recipe to the chicken they cook. While at Walton's Chicken, Boogie ran into Misty. "Misty, how are you" said Boogie. Misty responded that she was doing well. They both exchanges words of how each of them looked good. Misty and Boogie had an on and off

relationship during the time that he and Tameka

had broken-up. As a result, there is bad blood

between Misty and Tameka. Boogie hadn't seen

Misty in a few months, and they were both

happy to see one another. Boogie went against

his better judgement and sat at the table with

Misty. They ate lunch together and shared

several laughs together. Misty asked Boogie

when they would we have lunch together again?

Boogie just laughed and went on telling her how

he enjoyed the moment with her. She asked to

take a selfie and he agreed. He looked at this as

an innocent lunch with an old friend. Boogie,

being a gentleman, walked Misty one block

down the street to her cousin's house. He gave

Misty a hug and kissed her on her cheek before

leaving.

Boogie's got a call from his marijuana

connection. His connection told him that he had

something special for him. He picked Boogie up

in his new Mercedes truck. They discussed the

specifics while driving through the city. The

price was good, the quality, and the quantity

was good. This was going to be the best deal for

Boogie so far.

Boogie was now caught in a dilemma. On one

hand he could wait patiently for an uncertain job

or take this promising opportunity. Though he

attended the job fair, getting a call from any of the employers seemed doubtful. This opportunity would put Boogie in a good place financially. Boogie knew that he had all his people ready who could make this happen.

Though Boogie knew that his mother would do anything for him, he wanted to be able to take care of himself. In Boogie's mind, he was grown. Being grown meant being able to take care of himself. He had goals and dreams which he wanted to fulfill on his own. One of his goals was to move out of his mother's place and get an apartment.

Boogie made a drop off and got his people setup before heading to his girlfriend Tameka's house. She was there alone as her mother was at work. When Tameka opened the door, Boogie noticed the strange look that she had on her face. All he could think about was "what did I do?" Tameka quickly answered that question for him.

While Boogie thought that his lunch with Misty was innocent, misty had other plans. She decided to post the selfie that they took while eating. Misty put a post on one of the social media sites such as Facebook, Twitter, Instagram, or Snapchat, which Tameka ended up seeing. She added a caption that read "my old friend is a gentleman." Misty is also very

manipulative and planned to cause friction

between Boogie and Tameka.

"What's up with Misty, said Tameka?" Boogie

replied with "Misty who!" Tameka quickly

responded by saying "you know who Misty is!"

"Boy don't play!" Boogie tried to explain that

there was nothing going on with him and Misty,

Tameka wasn't hearing it. Boogie held

Tameka's hand and ensured her that she was the

one that he wanted. Tameka gently pushed

Boogie away. Boogie then held Tameka close

and looked at her with sincere eyes and told her

"I love you!" Tameka felt a warm feeling of

love in her heart but didn't want to give in that easy. Tameka turned to Boogie, with a tear in her eyes, and said "I can't do this any longer." "What do you mean" responded Boogie! They held each other for what seemed like an eternity. There were a few minutes of complete silence. When they let go, Boogie turned and walked out of her house.

Boogie felt disappointed that he was being accused of something that he didn't do. "There's nothing between me and Misty," he thought to himself. He also felt like it was him against the world. He had no job and now his girlfriend was against him. Well, at least that's what he felt.

Things always seem to go wrong at once.

Boogie left his girlfriend's house with an

attitude but was focused on making some

money. Everything went as planned. Boogie

made two flips on the first day and was planning

a third flip. His connection was excited and

provided him with his third package. Boogie

came back and felt like a champion as he was

prepared to move his third package on the first

day. Things appeared to be going well for the

first week. Money was starting to come faster

than he expected but there were no complaints

from Boogie. After a tiring night, Boogie

stopped by his friend Fred's house and ending up spending the night as it was getting late. Boogie got up early in the morning and called his mother to tell her good morning. He then went to picked up another package and it was back to the streets.

The block was on fire during that week. On the third day, Boogie came out to put his product on the street. When he came out, he noticed two suspicious guys walking down the block. Boogie remembers seeing the same two individuals a few days ago. "Hey Boogie, what's good" said one of the guys. Boogie responded by saying "do I know you?" "We need that good" the other guy responded.

Boogie told the guys that he didn't know what

they were talking about. It was something about

the two guys that rubbed Boogie the wrong way.

Boogie continued to walk away and felt very

suspicious of those two guys.

Things continued to go well for the rest of the

week. No one got robbed and everyone seemed

to be making money. As we know, all good

things must come to an end.

Boogie got up the next day and planned to

continue his money-making spree. When he

made it to the block, things felt different. A car

drove by slowly while looking at Boogie.

Boogie then walked in the opposite direction.

The same car returned a short time later. Boogie

saw the two suspicious guys as one of them

waved at him.

Boogie felt that something wasn't right and

decided that he needed to leave the area. As he

attempted to leave, a patrol car quickly

approached. Skerrrt! The loud sound of tires

coming to a sudden stop. Doors came open and

officers jumped out with their guns drawn.

Without hesitation, Boogie took off running as

fast as he could. At that point the chase was on.

FINDING

PURPOSE

Chapter 4

Back to the Chase

The chase continued for what appeared to be an eternity for Boogie. Knowing the geographical location of the neighborhood, gave Boogie a slight advantage and made it a little difficult for the police. He used this knowledge to his advantage as he ran through shortcuts, alleyways, and backyards. Boogie jumped a fence and attempted to hide behind a small dumpster. He suddenly heard one of the neighbor's dogs barking loudly at him. He then tried to shush the dog, but ole rover wasn't having it. Boogie knew that his cover would soon be blown, so he then started running again. He continued to run and run and run.

Boogie's advantage was short lived as he was getting more tired as he ran. Multiple patrol cars had joined the chase. Boogie was surrounded by officers and there was no way out. A patrol car pulled in front of him as he ran across a busy street. He slightly bumped into the car and

stumbled to the ground. He looked up and

quickly got up as he attempted to run. He

remembered the old saying "if you can look up,

you can get up." Boogie then felt a sharp pain in

his ankle as he took a few steps. A second patrol

car cut him off and he ran straight into that car.

He fell to the ground in agonizing pain and

grabbing his ankle. The first officer grabbed him

before he could get back to his feet. "Get on the

ground" the officer yelled. Other Officers

quickly grabbed him placing him face down on

the ground. They put hand cuffs on Boogie and

read him his rights. "You have the right to

remain silent. Anything you say can and will be

used against you." Boogie knew he was in trouble. He thought to himself, "what have I gotten myself into. My mother raised my better than this." Boogie felt uncertain as he didn't know what was going to happen next.

While in the patrol car on the way to the station, the officer started antagonizing Boogie. "We got you now!" "You're going to be put away for a long time" said the officer. "You people are the problem within our society." "Are you a drug dealer?" "All you guys do is sell drugs and kill one another" said the officer. Boogie quietly listened as the officer continued to speak with such disrespect. Boogie bit his tongue to keep from saying anything.

Boogie was taken to the police station and processed. They took his fingerprints and got all his information. They were surprised to find that he was only a juvenile. Boogie asked the officer "when can I make my phone call." Boogie called his mother to tell her the bad news. His mother yelled out "Nooooo, not my baby!" Her motherly instincts quickly kicked in as she started giving him encouraging words. She also shared a few words of advice with him. After hanging up the phone, she went to her room and started praying for her son. She was a woman of strong faith and believed that God would work things out for her son. She knew that she was going to attend her son's scheduled court hearing.

When Boogie walked into the courtroom, he was surprised to see both Misty and Tameka sitting there. Tameka and misty were both in court to show support for Boogie. Tameka sat next to Boogie's mother while Misty sat on the other end of the bench. They looked at one another with a look of resentment. They exchanged a few words and almost got into a fight on the way out. His mother was there with an attorney. The attorney moved the court to keep Boogie's case in the juvenile court system. To their surprise, Judge hardball granted his request.

His probation officer issued a violation of his probation for his resisting arrest and hindering prosecution. The prosecuting attorney wanted Boogie to serve time in a juvenile detention center. This was Boogie's third offense as a juvenile and they wanted to make an example of him. Boogie's attorney had a discussion with his probation officer and the state's attorney. After going back and forth, the prosecutor and his attorney eventually agreed to allow Boogie to attend a treatment program for juveniles. Judge

Hardball accepted the agreement and Boogie was sentenced to serve a one-year sentence for the violation and the arrest. After successfully completing the program, he would be released to his mother. Boogie and his mother were happy with his sentence. She believed that this program would help her son in making better decisions.

While in juvenile, Misty wrote Boogie one time and moved on with her life. Her letter consisted of the basic information and mostly entertaining him. Tameka consistently wrote and visited Boogie. Here letters consisted of information to help him grow into an adult. They shared a lot of laughs while at visitation. Boogie also had the

opportunity to apologize to Tameka for not

being the best that he could to her. They

appeared to be growing closer together as the

days went by. At one of the visits, Tameka had a

big surprise for Boogie. She told him that he

was a good person and would be a great dad. It

took Boogie a minute before he realized what

she was telling him. He then stood to his feet

and yelled "yeah." "I'm going to be a dad."

Boogie was overwhelmed with excitement, at

the news of Tameka being pregnant.

At this point, Boogie knew that life was more

than just about him. Now he would have to look

out for a child. A life, other than his own, that

he had to be responsible for. Just the thought of

being responsible for a child was kind of scary.

Boogie knew that he had to make some changes

in his life.

Chapter 5

Consequences

There are always consequences to our actions.

It's been nearly a month since the arrest. Boogie

started out the day with a good workout. He did

several sets of push-ups and sit-ups. Boogie felt

good after working off some stress and getting

sweaty. The workout put Boogie in a peaceful state of mind. After getting a shower, he would read letters from his mother and his girlfriend Tameka.

Boogie was excited about the book that his mother sent him. He tried to read a chapter each day. The book was a true story about a man who served a lot of time in prison and turned his life around after being released. "100 Years," is a must read for all young people. Boogie was inspired by the story and believed that he would do the same. One of the things that stood out to Boogie was how determined the man was. "The man didn't allow anything to stop him from achieving his goals. Any setbacks that he'd experienced, he came back stronger. When one employer told him "No," he went to the next. The man in the story appeared to be determined to accomplish his goals against all odds. Boogie was inspired by this story. Things were going well for this man and Boogie started to believe that he would achieve his goals also without committing any crime. Boogie enjoyed the book so much that he told as many others as he could.

While at the detention center, Boogie continued to reflect over his life and how things would be after his release. Boogie eventually grew to the point to where he felt more determined to make better decisions.

Nearly two months after being there, Boogie was called to one of the interview rooms. He was surprised to see his mother and two detectives waiting. His mother sat on one side of the table and two detectives sat on the other side of the table. He was called into one of the interview rooms. The officers had a serious and intimidating look on their faces. They began questioning him about a serious offense. "Do you know anything about a shooting that took place on 17th street?" After hearing those words Boogie had a blank stare on his face. He was surprised, as he never killed anyone. Though he been in plenty of fights, killing wasn't his cup of tea. The detectives were just fishing to see if he had information about an unsolved case. Boogie heard about the shooting like others had but he was in no way involved. After two hours of questioning, it was evident that Boogie had nothing to do with the case. Neither did he have any information regarding the case. He then returned to his dormitory.

Though there was beef in the hood, several years ago things were different. It was like one big community. Everyone got along from 1st street to 50th. One example is the story of

Boogie and Danny. Danny always had Boogie's back, and Boogie had Danny's back.

Boogie's mother and Ms. Pam, Danny's mother, remained friends. Though Boogie and Danny were childhood friends and grew up in the same neighborhood, things had changed over the years. Boogie remained true to the 20th posse while Danny started getting money with the 3rd street crew. No one really hated on him getting money, but the drug game will bring changes. It did appear that they were still friends but under the surface, things were different.

One day there was a big fight at the park between Danny and Boogie's best friend, Fred.

Danny got the best of Fred, but Fred held his

own. Boogie really took it personal as he felt

that Danny was attempting to impress his new

3rd street crew. Before things got out of hand

Boogie reached out to Danny. While on the

phone Boogie asked about the situation and

whether the beef was dead. Danny sounded

arrogant while on the phone. Danny responded

by saying "he was good but that it's whatever."

Though Boogie didn't like the outcome of the

fight between Danny and Fred, he charged it to

the game. Boogie understands the rules of the

street and a fair fight is a fair fight. There was a

lot of love and respect between Danny and

Boogie. Boogie disliked how their relationships changed, since they were all once close friends.

During the rest of the summer these two crews stayed in conflict. They went back and forth like never. One crew jumped someone from the other crew on one occasion. The other crew jumped on someone from the other crew on another occasion. Some of the fights were more serious than others. It was just heated between the two groups during the whole summer. During a basketball tournament in the Park, the 20th street crew wanted to attack Danny, but Boogie gave the command to stand-down.

On another occasion during the late-night hours, several loud gun shots were heard. Shortly after, the sound of paramedics and police sirens were heard. When the smoke cleared there were two young teenager who had gotten shot. Both had minor injuries. Boogie's girlfriend called him on the phone sounding hysterical. She was yelling at the top of her lungs "Fre-ee-ed goo-oot shot! Boogie said "who got shot. She repeated it, Fred got shot. Tears ran down her face. Boogie quickly dropped the phone before she could explain that Fred was not dead.

Fred was alive but in the hospital. The only thing that Boogie thought of was that this meant war. He thought that this was an attack from the 3rd street crew.

The detectives found that Fred was not the intended target. Jack was quickly arrested and confessed to the crime. Jack was an older guy from the 20th street area. The shooting was meant for Ivan. Ivan was one of the neighborhood stick-up kids. He earned his living by robbing drug dealers. He robbed a long list of individuals and he had many enemies.

It was proven that the shooting was not connected to the beef between the 20th and 3rd street crews. The word was still put out that the 3rd street crew was barred from coming anywhere beyond 15th street. Danny felt that this didn't include him, since he grew up in that hood. The truth of the matter was that Danny was no exception. Boogie gave Danny a call to inform him to steer clear of the hood for a while. Boogie told him that he couldn't hold off the wolves who wanted the head of anyone affiliated with the 3rd street crew. Danny was not hearing such a thing.

One day a group of individuals from the 3rd street hood, were leaving the Chinese restaurant on 17th street around 2am. Two masked gunmen approached and started shooting. When the smoke cleared four individuals were shot.

Though they were all in critical condition, they all escaped with their lives. The masked men ran in separate directions and were never capture.

A member of the 20th street crew was arrested but later released due to a lack of evidence. Danny then called Boogie to set-up a meeting and squash the beef. A meeting was planned but didn't take place due to Boogie getting arrested on the current charges.

FINDING

PURPOSE

Chapter 6

Lessons Learned

It's important to learn lessons in life. We sometimes learn through the consequences or rewards earned or simply by our experiences. Rewards sometimes encourage us to continue or improve a specific or celebrated behavior. On the other hand, consequences are usually meant to discourage a behavior, send a message, teach a lesson, or just for the sake of retribution. The message may be sent to an individual or sometimes to a group of individuals. There are cases in which lessons or consequences represent a principle or a standard that one must be live by. The thing about consequences is that we don't get to choose them. We must accept them as they come. This we must remember! If an individual punch another person in the face, consequences may soon follow. The reality is that the consequences may far outweigh being punched back in the face.

In Boogie's case, it was necessary for him to learn a life lesson about being in the streets. If he doesn't change, things aren't going to end well for him. The streets didn't have his best interest in mind. The streets will consume anyone in its path, and he wasn't an exception to this rule. The streets had him on a highway to prison or an early death. Boogie had a lot of potential and could do more with his life.

Boogie was kind of shook up when he was questioned about the shooting. In Boogie's mind, being questioned about or even associated with a shooting was a serious offense. Boogie thought that it was unfair that he was being questions about a shooting when he had nothing

to do with it. A charge of this nature may cause

an individual to be incarcerated for a very long

time. Boogie knew this was a serious offense

and was thankful that his name would be

cleared.

While in juvenile, Boogie got the report that

things were getting more dangerous in the

neighborhood. Fighting one another is one thing

but shooting was another ball game. Boogie had

to take a serious look at himself and decide what

he wanted for his life. This called for him to

reflect honestly over his life. This was a time for

Boogie to choose between life and death. This

was a time to make a decision that may change

the course of the rest of his life. In addition to

his own life, Boogie had to think about being a

dad.

Boogie's thought back to when he was younger.

His Uncle Gus was somewhat of a positive role

model for him when he was around 10. It may

be safe to say that his uncle was the only father

figure that he ever knew. He taught Boogie how

to throw and catch a football. He signed him up

to play little league football one year. He took

Boogie to different sporting events. He used to

encourage Boogie to make something good out

of his life. He went to the school with Boogie to

speak to his teacher on several occasions. His Uncle used to tell Boogie that he wouldn't allow the streets to take him. Boogie was thinking of how life may have been better for him had his Uncle Gus still been alive. He felt that he would've benefited from his guidance.

Being in lock up allowed Boogie the needed time to sit down and think about his life. This may have been a good thing for Boogie. Sitting in an institution was the last place he wanted to be. While thinking, he heard the Officer call his name for mail. After walking to the officer who was passing out mail, he was happy to see that it was another letter from Tameka. As usual, he

took the letter back to his cell to read it in peace.

FINDING

PURPOSE

Chapter 7

Purpose

Sometimes finding purpose, in all the daily

madness, may be a difficult task. At the same

time, hidden behind the darkness and confusion

of reality, may exist a glare of hope. Sometimes

hope can be found in the smallest of packages.

Boogie's girlfriend Tameka was in the hospital

as her due date was closely approaching.

Tameka's mother and Boogie's mother were

both there to offer support. The doctor urged her

to pushed but she continued to moan in pain.

She responded by saying "I Can't." "Yes, you

can" said the doctor! Now just push. She finally

found the strength to push several times and

eventually the miracle happened. The doctor

yelled out "it's a boy!" The bringing forth of life

is a miracle. Though Tameka had a painful

birth, to see her child brought joy to her heart.

It was like a sigh of relief as Tameka laid her

head back on the bed. Tameka's mother asked,

"What are you going to name the baby?"

Tameka looked at her mother and responded,

"my baby's name is going to be "Purpose." Both

Tameka's mother and Boogie's mother looked

at Tameka in awe. Boogie's mother responded

"Purpose," I love that name. Tameka's mothers

said, that's a great name. They both then started

hugging Tameka. Her mother told her to get

some rest and she fell asleep.

The day that Boogie got released from lock-up,

his mother drove him to Tameka's house. He

ran fast as he could to her front door. When

Tameka's mother opened the door, he quickly

spoke and ran through the door and up the stairs.

He ran so fast that she could barely hear him speak to her. While coming up the stairs he asked, "where is purpose?" Tameka responded, he's in here with me. He then entered her room and saw his son "purpose" asleep in Tameka's arms. He picked up his one and only child and kissed him on the face. He quietly told him that he loved him. He then promised his son "purpose" that he would never leave him again.

Tameka said that his name is purpose and he responded by saying I already know. I love that name "purpose" said Boogie. Things felt different for Boogie. Boogie was overwhelmed with the fact that he was now a dad. He was also happy to be out of that juvenile facility.

Boogie's mother told him that he had a job offer at a local warehouse. Things appeared to be working out for Boogie. Boogie's mother was full of joy as she knew that her prayers were answered.

What is life without purpose? Life without purpose isn't a life at all. Kind of like travelling without knowing the destination. This is like having a fling with someone without meaning. No feelings involved, just a cheap thrill that runs out the moment it's over.

On the other hand, a life with purpose is full of

potential to help another. On the other hand, a

life without purpose is full of trouble. As the

song goes "you can get with this or you can get

with that." Life is about choices. Sometimes it is

better to learn life's lessons the hard way.

Experience is the best teacher. Well, this is true

in Boogie's case.

With a new child and a real "purpose" in his

life, Boogie knew that he must be more

responsible. He must be more responsible to

himself as a young man. He must be more

responsible to his newborn child as a father. He

must also decide whether he will continue to be

a man and a spouse to his child's mother,

Tameka. Life is about choices and it is all up to

Boogie. What will Boogie do after finding

purpose? Will he continue living on the right

path and making responsible choices? On the

other hand, will he go back to his old self?

Boogie can now say that he's learned a lot

during this journey. Some of his experiences

had the potential of causing him to continue

making excuses. Some of his lessons may have

caused him to put up defense mechanisms and

blame others. Instead of making excuses and

blaming others, Boogie learned that he must

continue to evaluate his own life and make the

necessary adjustments. He also learned to keep things in perspective. This means that he is learning to appreciating the things that he has. Tameka was a blessing to him and now he is starting to see the light. Boogie is now learning to take the time to think about how things will positively or negatively affect his son.

Boogie has gained strength by going through several different forms of trials and tribulations. This was his way of finding purpose. It has been two-fold for Boogie. He found purpose in his life by finding his son "purpose!"

FINDING

PURPOSE

A Year Later

A year later, Boogie reflects over his life as he plays with his only son "purpose." Boogie looked straight ahead, as if he is looking at a camera or caught in deep thought. He seemed to be happy with his life. He was especially excited to be a dad to his son. This was an opportunity for Boogie to be the dad to his son and give his son something that he never had, a dad. Boogie is thankful for another chance in life. He now understands that things must change in his life for him to be a good dad. He decided not to hang out on the streets with his friends. Most of his time will be dedicated to his son. Though

Boogie received support from his mother, girlfriend, and school counselor, it took for him to make the changes in his life.

Can't be such a good dad if he were to return to lock-up. Boogie heard how several individuals from the 20th street crew were sent to prison. It broke Boogie's heart to hear how two of his close friends were killed in a drive-by shooting. Boogie sent his condolence to both of their mothers.

It seems that Boogie walked away from the street life, just in time. Boogie's school counselor helped him get involved in volunteering. Boogie became a community volunteer on the weekends for a well-known

organization. Boogie became employee of the

month at his warehouse job. He enjoyed

stocking shelves and earning an honest living.

He went on to earn his High School Diploma.

Boogie and his girlfriend Tameka decided to

pursue more of a committed relationship with

each other. They are growing together as they

learn how to be parents to their son "purpose."

Boogie's friend Fred is also considering giving

up the street life also. He volunteered on one

occasion during one of those weekends with

Boogie. Maybe Boogie may influence him to

change his life one day. Well, Fred will have to

make up his own mind just as Boogie made up his mind. Boogie's mother decided to attend church services more often as God has answered most of her many prayers. Boogie's purpose is to live a productive life and be a father to his son! In the process he may even be a good example to others.

A Word from the Author

(Mark L Baynard is a self-published author. Though this is his first work of fiction, this is the fourth book that he's written. Mark writes from the heart and attempts to deliver hope and value to others. Writing about things close to his heart is the zone he works best in.)

As the author of this book, I have a few things for the readers to think about. Purpose will assist us in this journey of life. Finding purpose is an ongoing process. What is your purpose you ask? Well let's try to answer a few questions. What drives you more than anything else in the world? What makes you happy? These are just

some of the questions to answer in the process
of finding purpose.

Life without purpose can be full of trouble and
hardship. To find purpose is understanding the
reason behind what and why a person does
things. More specifically, finding purpose is
understanding the reason for your existence. No
one should do anything without clearly knowing
why they did it. Purpose is the reason why we
do the things that we do.

Though Boogie is a fictional character in this
story, there are many Boogie's in our society.
Feeling confused and searching for
understanding.

Being confused can be an unsafe place to remain in. This place will be unsafe for the individual and those closest to that individual.

As an author, I'm not attempting to redefine the meaning of purpose or how to find it. I just wanted to put it into the form of a story. I wanted to make it clear for the average reader to understand that finding purpose is necessary. Stories have a way of painting things clearer than words alone. Stories allow readers to relate to or even see themselves in the middle of the action. I believe that it is necessary for our youth and adults to have purpose to steer clear of some of the many pitfalls that they may face.

Purpose may give us something to stand on and stand for. We live in a world where our children are sometimes more subject to abuse, drugs, gangs, and incarceration. Knowing our Purpose will put us in a better position to assist our youth in addressing those challenges. Sometimes it may only take a few encouraging words or a kind gesture to brighten another's day.

Lacking purpose in my own life when I was a teenager, led me to experience unnecessary hardships. Drugs use, crime, abuse, and prison were all a part of my past. Things didn't improve for me until I started finding purpose in my life. I was then able to see success in my life. Sometimes, we may feel that, the only way for us to feel successful is to live through the success of others. This can be a very unhealthy state to live in because it prevents an individual from reaching their full potential or goals. It's good to support others in reaching their goals but try not to live through that.

While attempting to describe purpose, it may be easier to establish two categories: the "who" and the "what." Purpose has to do with who we are more than what we are. The "who" is internal and can't be visualized by others. This consists of our values, identity, and character. Purpose allows us to understand why these things were established and creates a strong foundation.

The "what" is external and can be, in most cases, visually observed by others. This will include our financial status, position on the job, car we drive, house we live in, and other materialistic possessions.

I think that finding purpose will help us identify the who we are and bring out the very best in us. Finding purpose will add a greater cause to an individual's life. Each day we wake up in the morning, think about the purpose that you have for living.

Though our purpose may be a very minute (my-Noot) part of the big picture or puzzle in life, it's necessary. To find purpose in life is to gain a clear understanding of why we're here. What moves us and why we do the things we do. This will answer some of the questions that we have about life. I believe that this is the point in which more value is added to our lives. We are then able to more effectively help others along this journey. Continue to find purpose in and for your life. This is a process that will continue for the rest of our lives. Find Purpose in your life!

www.ingramcontent.com/pod-product-compliance
Lightning Source LLC
Chambersburg PA
CBHW071405170626
46811CB00003B/1272